❚QUICKREADS

SOMETHING DREADFUL DOWN BELOW

ANNE SCHRAFF

QUICKREADS

SERIES 1
Black Widow Beauty
Danger on Ice
Empty Eyes
The Experiment
The Kula'i Street Knights
The Mystery Quilt
No Way to Run
The Ritual
The 75-Cent Son
The Very Bad Dream

SERIES 2
The Accuser
Ben Cody's Treasure
Blackout
The Eye of the Hurricane
The House on the Hill
Look to the Light
Ring of Fear
The Tiger Lily Code
Tug-of-War
The White Room

SERIES 3
The Bad Luck Play
Breaking Point
Death Grip
Fat Boy
No Exit
No Place Like Home
The Plot
Something Dreadful Down Below
Sounds of Terror
The Woman Who Loved a Ghost

SERIES 4
The Barge Ghost
Beasts
Blood and Basketball
Bus 99
The Dark Lady
Dimes to Dollars
Read My Lips
Ruby's Terrible Secret
Student Bodies
Tough Girl

www.sdlback.com

Copyright ©2010, 2002 by Saddleback Educational Publishing
All rights reserved. No part of this book may be reproduced or transmitted in any form or by any means, electronic or mechanical, including photocopying, recording, or by any information storage and retrieval system, without the written permission of the publisher.

ISBN-13: 978-1-61651-205-7
ISBN-10: 1-61651-205-9
eBook: 978-1-60291-927-3

Printed in Guangzhou, China
0411/04-80-11

15 14 13 12 11   2 3 4 5 6

■ ■ ■

Augusto Goleta could fix just about anything on wheels. Even as a kid in the Philippines he'd worked on his father's jeepney, a minibus taxi. Just five years ago, the family had moved to the United States. Now Gus was living in his own apartment in the city. Everything was fine—except for one small problem. Mr. Devorka, the manager of the building, kept snakes.

"It gives me the creeps that Mr. Devorka keeps snakes," Gus complained to his girlfriend, Melita.

Melita giggled and said, "I didn't think you were afraid of *anything!*"

Gus shrugged, embarrassed by his fear.

But he really *was* worried about Devorka's little hobby. What if he woke up some night and found snakes in his room! He shuddered to think of it.

Gus had one good friend in the apartment building—his next door neighbor, Jack Hunter. Tonight they planned to watch a football game on Jack's new 60-inch TV. The little old lady across the hall, Mrs. Duncan, might complain if they got loud. Then they'd quiet down. Old Mrs. Duncan reminded Gus of his own *lola,* his grandmother. Back in the Philippines, she too had spied on everybody in the family compound. These days *lola* lived with Gus's parents in America.

Sometimes, when he visited his family, Gus brought back some *lumpia* for Mrs. Duncan. "My *lola* made this for you," he'd say.

■ ■ ■

Gus had a busy day. He fixed a fuel pump in one car, and put a rebuilt tranny in another. He tuned up several more cars and worked overtime. He was glad for the extra money. It meant that he and Melita could be married that much sooner.

When he came home from work, Gus hurried down the hall and rang Jack's doorbell. The football game was about to start. Gus was surprised when no one answered. "Hey, Jack!" he shouted. "It's almost time for the game!"

The door across the hall opened and Mrs. Duncan peered out—as usual. "He didn't come home from work today," she said. "Your friend always whistles when he comes down the hall. But I didn't hear any whistling today."

"Yeah?" Gus said. "We're supposed to watch a football game in a few minutes." Impatiently, Gus hit the bell again. Nothing happened.

"Something funny's going on over there," Mrs. Duncan said. "I heard weird sounds this morning. It upset me so much I couldn't digest my oatmeal."

Gus stared at the door of Jack's apartment, suddenly afraid.

■ ■ ■

"*Jack! You in there?*" he shouted again. He turned the knob, but the door was locked. "Maybe he got sick or something and passed out."

Mrs. Duncan frowned. "I don't know," she said as she was closing her own door, "but I don't like it one bit."

Gus sighed and went downstairs to Mr. Devorka's apartment. It was in the basement. It made his skin crawl to go anywhere near that snake pit, but somebody had to check on Jack.

As he headed downstairs, Gus's imagination began working overtime. Maybe one of those snakes had gotten out and come crawling up into Jack's apartment. Maybe the poor guy had been bitten! It was *possible*. This rotting old building was riddled with cracks and holes. If the rent wasn't so cheap, Gus would have moved out a long time ago.

Devorka denied that any of his snakes

were poisonous—but Gus always had suspected the man was lying.

Gus rang the door bell. "Yeah?" came the raspy, deep voice from inside the apartment. Devorka was lazy. He didn't like to be bothered.

"It's Gus Goleta," Gus called through the closed door. "My friend, Jack Hunter, isn't answering his door. We were supposed to watch the football game tonight. I'm worried."

"So? What am I supposed to do about it?" Devorka demanded.

"I thought you could open Jack's door and check on him," Gus said. "Mrs. Duncan said she heard weird sounds in there this morning."

"That old busybody is always imagining things," Devorka growled as he opened the door. Inside, Gus could see snakes in stacked cages against the far wall. He was revolted. "Jack Hunter is a no-good punk," Devorka grumbled. "He's probably just out chasing girls and raising cain."

"Maybe—but I still think you need to

check," Gus insisted.

Devorka grabbed his heavy ring of keys and went up the stairs ahead of Gus. "I'm not supposed to be going into tenants' apartments, you know," he complained.

"If you'll just open the door, I'll go in and check," Gus said. "Maybe Jack fell and hit his head or something. He might need help. He won't mind me checking up on him."

"It's against the law," Devorka said stubbornly. "I shouldn't be doing this. I could get in a lotta trouble."

As soon as they reached Jack's apartment, Mrs. Duncan's door opened a crack. She kept the chain on, but Gus could see her peering out. "Something is wrong over there," she called out. "I can feel it in my bones. Something bad has happened to your friend Jack!"

Devorka grumbled under his breath, "Old witch! She makes me sick. Why doesn't she mind her own business?"

Gus looked around the apartment. It seemed to be empty. For some reason, he had a strange feeling that he might never see Jack Hunter again.

■ ■ ■

"Jack?" Gus called out. He didn't really expect his friend to answer—and he didn't.

"Be quick about this," Devorka said. "I tell you I don't like it! We're breaking into somebody's apartment."

Gus hurried to the bedroom. The bed was unmade, and there was a large brownish stain on the rug! Just last week Gus had helped Jack bring in a new mattress. The ugly stain hadn't been there then.

"What's that stain?" Gus asked.

Devorka snorted rudely. "He spilled coffee there, the slob. He said he'd get it cleaned. Have you seen enough? Let's get out of here now. The guy is out carousing—that's all."

Gus went to his own apartment and called the computer repair store where Jack worked. They said he hadn't shown up for work today and didn't even call. Gus was worried. That wasn't like Jack!

Then Gus called Jack's latest girlfriend, Dawn Stonehatter.

When a woman answered, he said, "Hi, this is Gus Goleta, Jack's friend."

"Oh, yes," she said. "You're the cute Filipino guy I met when we all went to Disneyland."

"Listen—Jack and I were going to watch football tonight. Do you know where he is? I called his work and they said he didn't show up there, either. I'm—uh—concerned," Gus said.

"Is his car parked in its regular space?" Dawn asked.

"Man!" Gus cried. "Why didn't I think of that? I'll get back to you, Dawn."

Gus rushed outside. None of the tenants had garages. They just had assigned places in the parking lot. Jack's nice new car was assigned a spot on one end, and Gus's beat-up old clunker had a spot at the other end.

Jack's car was in its space. Gus tried the door, but it was locked. He peered inside.

Jack even had the security iron clamped across the wheel. He was a real cautious guy.

A sick feeling came over Gus again. Once, when he'd been a small boy in the Philippines, his pet dog disappeared. His parents and his brothers and sisters said not to worry. They thought the little dog had wandered off and would return soon. But Gus knew better. For some reason he *knew* that his dog wouldn't come back—that something *bad* had happened to him. Right now, that was how Gus felt about Jack Hunter.

It was like the earth had swallowed up his friend.

■ ■ ■

Back in the apartment, Gus called Dawn again. "Dawn, his car is parked where it should be. Something must have happened this morning."

"Now you've got *me* worried," Dawn said. "I'm coming right over, okay?"

Gus hung up. He didn't know Dawn very well, but Jack seemed to be crazy about her. On her birthday Jack had given her a beautiful diamond necklace. Gus wondered how Jack managed it. His job didn't pay as well as Gus's did!

Dawn arrived about 20 minutes later. She wasn't as upset as Gus was. "I'm sure there's a good explanation for this," she said confidently.

"I'm scared, Dawn. I think we should call the police and report that Jack is missing," Gus said.

"Oh, that would really be jumping the gun!" she said. "When Jack comes sauntering in, we'll feel foolish."

"But I've got this gut feeling that he's been hurt," Gus insisted.

"Jack wouldn't want us to panic," Dawn said. "Look—I've got a key to his apartment. Let's go inside and check it out. He had a couple of projects going. Maybe he went to check on them."

Gus was surprised. "What kind of projects, Dawn?" he asked. "Jack never told me about any projects."

Suddenly Dawn seemed nervous. She twisted the straps on her handbag. "Uh—he's consulting or something. I'm not really sure." But Gus noticed that her eyes looked narrow and sly—as if she were hiding something.

"Is Jack doing something illegal?" Gus asked.

"No—oh, no! He and some guys on the Internet are just importing things. They bring in stuff and ship it out. You know—without going through all the red tape. They kinda go through the back doors," she explained.

Gus was alarmed. "He's not in the drug business, is he?" he asked.

"Drugs? Oh, no! Oh, wow, Gus, *no!* He's just importing stuff with some guys. You know how the government is—how they make you jump through all these hoops. I mean, a person can hardly do business anymore without the government butting in."

As Dawn unlocked the door to Jack's apartment, Gus told her about Mrs. Duncan hearing weird noises this morning. "Oh, that old snoop! Jack hates her!" Dawn said. Then she sat down at Jack's computer. Gus watched over her shoulder as she started to read Jack's e-mail messages.

Hi, Jacko. Ready to sell Boomer and the Missus. Mike.

Gus was bewildered. "What's that mean?" he asked.

Dawn jumped at his tone of voice. "Nothing," she stammered.

"You're *lying!*" Gus snapped. "I'm calling the police!"

■ ■ ■

Dawn grabbed his arm. "Oh, please don't!" she cried. "I'm sure that Jack is okay. He must have gone somewhere with Mike. If you call the police, you could get him in trouble!"

Gus was torn between his fear for Jack and this girl's persuasive pleading. "Okay, we'll hold off for now," Gus said. "But Jack better show up pretty soon, or I'm making a report."

After Dawn left, Gus tried to catch the last of the football game on his own TV. It wasn't a very good game. As he shut it off, he heard an unsettling sound from down below. It sounded like a pick axe stabbing into hard ground in the basement!

When Gus stepped out in the hall, Mrs. Duncan opened her door. Gus couldn't help smiling. She didn't miss a thing. The poor lady was so lonely she had to spend half her life at the door, waiting for something to happen. "Do you hear it, too?" she asked softly.

"Yeah, coming from the basement," Gus said. "I wonder what ol' Devorka is doing down there now?"

"I don't like that man," Mrs. Duncan said. "He gives me the willies. Who would want to live down there with all those snakes?"

"Yeah, he creeps me out, too," Gus said. "I'm going to see what he's doing." Then Gus remembered something. He asked Mrs. Duncan to describe the strange sounds she'd heard from Jack's apartment this morning.

"Some woman, yelling and crying," Mrs. Duncan said.

Gus was surprised. Was Dawn here this morning? But wouldn't she have mentioned that? "Did you see the woman, Mrs. Duncan?" Gus asked.

"Oh, yes," she said. "It was that little blonde he's taken up with. I think she's a gold digger. At first she was yelling at him at the top of her lungs. Then she quieted down and hurried off. After that, I didn't hear anything."

Gus was confused. Did Dawn and Jack have a fight? Could *she* have hurt him? Gus couldn't imagine that. But still—if she had nothing to hide, why didn't she say that she'd seen Jack?

Gus felt his skin crawling as he went down to the basement. His imagination was running wild. Had Devorka killed Jack? Was he burying him in the dirt floor at the far corner of the basement?

When Gus rang Devorka's bell, the man

shouted from another part of the basement. "Who's there?"

"Gus Goleta. What's all the noise about?" Gus called out.

Devorka came around a corner. His clothes were dirty, and he was carrying a pick axe. "I'm planting mushrooms," he said. "What's it to you?" He didn't ask if Jack had returned. Perhaps he already knew the answer.

■ ■ ■

Devorka followed Gus up the stairs, the pick axe still in hand.

"Listen, Goleta, you get something straight, okay? Your buddy is a punk, and he just took off, got it?"

"Yeah, sure," Gus said, anxious to get away from the man *and* the axe.

"His girlfriend called me a little while ago," Devorka said. "She knows where Hunter is. That's what the chick said, anyway. So look—there's no big mystery, okay? Just let it alone."

Gus gasped in shock. Did Dawn Stonehatter really call Devorka? Or was the old man making up the story to calm Gus's suspicions?

Once again Gus had to consider the possibility that Dawn had something to do with Jack's disappearance. Maybe she and Devorka were working together somehow.

Back in his apartment, Gus lay on the bed, staring at the walls and ceiling. There were holes all over. There was even a fair-sized hole between his apartment and Jack's. Gus wished he'd been home this morning. He could have peered through the hole and seen what was going on between Dawn and Jack.

Gus was tired, but his thoughts were racing. Maybe Jack was doing something illegal and the cops got him. Gus knew that Jack didn't have high standards. He often talked about stealing stuff from his company. It was small stuff, but still— Gus would never have done anything like that. Jack could easily have been in on something crooked.

Then Gus was suddenly wide awake. He felt something pressing down on his feet! Sitting up and peering toward the foot of the bed, he gasped in horror.

Something was moving on the bed!

It was wriggling over the blankets....

It was a snake—a *large* snake! Gus made a helpless, strangled sound of terror. As the snake turned, Gus could see its tapered head lifting up. *The snake was coming toward Gus's head.*

Gus wanted to run. But he was afraid the snake would detect the motion and strike at him. He remembered reading that snakes strike at moving objects.

Gus was bathed in cold sweat. He felt paralyzed. But how could he just lie there, waiting for his life to be snuffed out?

■ ■ ■

Gus couldn't hold back. He leaped from the bed, hurling the blankets against the approaching reptile. When his bare feet hit the floor, he couldn't believe that he had actually gotten away. He stood there, shaking and groaning, as the snake slithered out of the bedding.

Gus snatched up his old bathrobe, grabbed the phone, and called Devorka. His eyes still on the snake, he screamed into the phone, "Devorka, get up here fast! One of your dirty snakes got in my bed! I almost had a heart attack, man!"

"Stay cool, I'm coming," Devorka said. But he sounded frightened. In minutes, he was at the door with a sack and a snake-catching pole.

Gus yelled at him. "I'm telling you, man, it's not *right* to keep dangerous snakes where people live. It's just plain wrong! It's illegal!"

Approaching the snake cautiously, Devorka snatched it up with the tongs and dropped it into the sack.

"How come you're so careful, if your snakes aren't venomous?" Gus cried.

"A snakebite is nasty—even the bite of a harmless snake," Devorka said. "Look, kid,

I'm really sorry about this. None of my snakes has ever escaped before. All of my cages are very secure."

"Then how did that thing get in here?" Gus demanded.

Devorka shifted from one foot to the other, breathing hard. "It must have been one of the snakes your friend stole from me. I bet it came through that hole over there. It's just a harmless colubrid snake—not one of my better ones. But your pal thought it was a good one, so he stole it.

"I found out he cooked up some business on the Internet. Some guys offered big bucks for breeding pairs of rare snakes. I told him I'd turn him in if he didn't return the snakes he stole from me. I thought he'd given them all back. But he must have lost the colubrid. Maybe it's been hiding in his closet. Then it must have come over here—"

Gus stared at Devorka in disbelief. "Jack was *stealing* your snakes? Come on, Devorka! That's hard to swallow."

"Well, I got some pretty valuable ones, you

know. There are green pythons and— Anyway, kid, I want to make sure there's no hard feelings. How about you skip next month's rent to make up for what happened? Deal?" Devorka said.

"Okay," Gus said. "But I better not see another snake in here!"

Gus didn't believe Jack stole the snake. It must have crawled up from the snake pit in the basement. But he was absolutely sure about one thing. As soon as he used up that free month's rent, Gus was moving out of this rathole!

■ ■ ■

Gus hoped he'd get a call from Jack at work the next day. But no call came. After thinking about it, Gus realized that there had been a change in Jack over the past few months. Gus had never said anything, but he felt Dawn was bad for Jack. She was greedy. Gus sensed that Dawn was always pressuring Jack to buy her things and take her to expensive places. In the past four months, Jack seemed to develop an almost desperate need for money.

When Gus got home from work, Dawn called. "We have to talk," she said. "Could you come over to my apartment?"

"Sure," Gus said. He took down her address, figuring that Dawn must have news about Jack.

Gus wasn't surprised to find that Dawn lived in an upscale neighborhood of fine new apartments. Jack was clearly out of his league when he dated the girl.

Dawn answered Gus's knock immediately. She motioned for him to sit beside her on the couch. "I have a confession to make, Gus. I didn't tell you the whole truth before. Sorry—but I was too scared. The thing is that Mike Devorka and Jack were in business together. They were buying and selling rare snakes. Some of the breeds were just about extinct. And a person can go to prison for a long time for dealing in endangered animals, you know."

Gus remembered the cryptic e-mail

message he'd read on Jack's computer. So "Mike" was old Devorka! What was the "boomer"? It had to be a snake—part of a breeding pair.

"I've talked to Devorka and I don't believe him anymore," Dawn said. "I think something bad *did* happen to Jack, and Devorka knows about it."

Gus glared at the girl, angry at her for pushing Jack into his criminal enterprise. "Dawn, you never told me you were there yesterday morning. Why were you fighting with Jack? Were you demanding more jewelry?"

"Oh, please!" Dawn whimpered. "Don't talk to me like that, Gus! I feel bad enough already. I never told Jack to get into that rotten business with Devorka. Is it *my* fault if he wanted to shower me with gifts? Yeah, we had an argument yesterday. But that was because he weaseled out of taking me to Hawaii for the weekend. I guess I got a little emotional."

"So, you were maybe the last person to see Jack," Gus said. "Maybe you were the last person to see him *alive,* Dawn! But you've lied all along. How do I know you're not lying now?"

Dawn looked shocked. "Surely you don't think *I* hurt Jack!" she gasped.

"I don't know what I think," Gus said wearily. "All I know is that I'm calling the police. It's way past time I did that."

Dawn nodded. Tears were streaming down her face.

■ ■ ■

Gus drove home, planning to call the police from his apartment. He wanted them to meet him there. He felt sick. But there still was no positive evidence that his friend was dead.

As Gus walked down the hall, he rang Jack's bell again. He didn't expect an answer, but suddenly the door swung open. It was Devorka, a cheerful smile on his face. "I'm cleaning up in here. Gotta make the place look good for the next tenant. I got a call from Hunter, by the way. He's in Mexico, fishing.

25

Can you beat that?"

Gus studied the man's expression. He was lying. It was written all over his ugly face. Gus could see it in his narrowed pig eyes. But he didn't say anything.

Devorka followed Gus to his own door. "Yeah, the guy is fishing in Mexico. Lot of sharks down there. So if he doesn't come back, we'll know what happened to him, right?"

Gus could tell that Devorka was building a story—something that would explain why Jack wouldn't be returning from his fishing trip. *Ever.* "Hey, kid, you look funny. What are you thinking?"

"Nothing," Gus said. "I've had a hard day. I want to go in and take a shower."

"That's a lie! I can see that you aren't buying my story, kid. You've got that fish-eyed look," Devorka said.

"Sure I'm buying it. Jack is in Mexico fishing," Gus said. He was struggling to keep the suspicion off his face. The truth was he was desperately eager to get on the phone with the police.

Now it all seemed obvious. Devorka had killed Jack and buried him in the basement. And if Gus didn't play his cards right, he'd be next. Gus had always known there was something dreadful in the basement. Now he knew how really dreadful it was.

"I'm not buying it," Devorka said.

"I told you I had a hard day," Gus said. "I just want to rest."

Gus and Devorka both noticed Mrs. Duncan's door opening a crack. "Mind your own business, you old crone!" Devorka growled. "People are sick of you spying on them. Shut your door or I'll double your rent!"

Mrs. Duncan hastily closed the door, and Devorka returned his attention to Gus. "You are gonna call the cops, right?" he hissed.

"Don't be silly," Gus stammered as he unlocked his door.

Suddenly, Devorka pulled out a gun and jabbed it into Gus's back. "We're going downstairs *now*," he said.

■ ■ ■

Devorka followed Gus down the stairs. Gus's heart was pounding, and his mouth was so dry he almost choked. What could he do? He didn't think he could yell if he tried.

They reached the door of the basement apartment. "Open up and go on inside," Devorka snapped.

The sight of the snakes writhing in their cages sent fresh chills down Gus's spine. He felt sick and dizzy.

"Just let me go, and I'll forget about everything!" Gus cried out desperately.

"Yeah, sure," Devorka laughed. "You know too much and you've guessed the rest. Hunter and I were partners in the snake business—but he was a fool. He didn't know how to handle the snakes, not the venomous ones. But he wouldn't admit what an idiot he was!"

A numb feeling crept over Gus's body. So one of the snakes *had* gotten Jack!

"I came home and found him down here," Devorka went on. "He'd been packing the venomous boomslang in his apartment. Then the snake bit him and he bled on the rug. So he came down here looking for help. He was sick and wanted to go to the emergency room. But if we had called 911, the whole thing would have been out in the open."

Gus was horrified. "So you just let him die?" he gasped.

"I wasn't going to blow the deal sky high," Devorka said in a flat voice. "I didn't kill Jack Hunter. The snake did. But I'm the one who would have gotten the blame."

"But you might have saved his life!" Gus groaned.

"I'm *not* a murderer! The snake killed him. I didn't mean for it to happen. I just buried him after he stopped breathing. What else could I do? Now everything is messed up for me. Listen, Goleta: You go over there and get in that closet *fast*. I want a head start out of here before you call the cops," Devorka said.

Gus opened the closet door and reluctantly went inside. The dark little room was filled with dirt and cobwebs. Devorka tossed a sack in after Gus. Then he slammed and locked the door.

"I'm sorry, kid," Devorka said. "I never could have shot you. Believe me, I'm not a murderer. But you know too much. It's better this way."

Gus was bewildered by what the man was saying. But then the sack Devorka had thrown in the closet *began to move*. Even in the darkness, Gus could see the hideous snake emerge from the bag, its poisonous fangs ready to strike.

Gus started to scream—but his cries were quickly drowned out by police sirens. In just a few moments, two officers yanked open the closet door. "The lady across the hall called us," one cop explained. The other was handcuffing Devorka.

■ ■ ■

That night, Gus gave Mrs. Duncan a big hug. "Now I have two lolas," he told her. The old lady looked surprised and very pleased. Gus owed a lot to Mrs. Duncan. Right then and there he resolved that she would not be so lonely anymore. He'd take her out once in a while and visit often. She could count on it.

After-Reading Wrap-Up

1. What is the "something dreadful" from the title? Where is "down below"?

2. What does Devorka say when he insists that he's not responsible for Jack's death? Do you think Devorka was right? Why or why not?

3. Who is the most important person in *Something Dreadful Down Below?* Who is the hero?

4. How did the snake probably get into Gus' room?

5. Gus felt Jack didn't have high standards. What did he mean by that?

6. Describe Dawn in a short paragraph.